What is philosophy?

Noodle Juice Ltd
www.noodle-juice.com
Stonesfield House, Stanwell Lane, Great Bourton, Oxfordshire, OX17 1QS
First published in Great Britain 2023
Copyright © Noodle Juice Ltd 2023
Text by Noodle Juice 2022 • Illustrations by Katie Rewse 2022
All rights reserved
Printed in China
A CIP catalogue record of this book is available from the British Library
ISBN: 978-1-915613-67-7
10 9 8 7 6 5 4 3 2 1

What is life?

To be able to move...

To be alive or have life means to be able to eat...

To be able to grow...

What does it mean to be human?

There are many human beings living on this planet. A human being is a person. A person like YOU, who breathes in air, who sleeps and eats and enjoys being with other people.

But that is also true of some animals. What makes humans different?

We can **think**, we can **read**.
We wear **clothes**, we use **money**.
We show we **care** for one another.
We are unique, we **choose**.

What makes us happy?

Enough food to eat and

somewhere **warm** to sleep!

Smiles.

Being **grateful**.

Sharing things.

People who **care** about us and who we care about.

Music.

Sunshine.

Looking after our bodies; exercise, sleep and **eating well.**

Learning things.

Building things.

Making things.

Spending time with family and **friends.**

What is love?

When you LOVE someone, you care about how they feel. You want to spend time with them and you trust them.

Love for a parent or a pet, a best friend or a grandparent can feel different. You can love a favourite book or favourite food, but when you love someone, it feels GOOD to be with them.

What is truth?

Truth is **fact**, truth is real.

Truth can be **seen**.

Truth is **not made up** and truth is not a lie.

Believing **lies** can spoil things or hurt people.

Being truthful is a **good thing**.

Truth is not an opinion, or what you think about something, but it is TRUE that people can have different opinions and that is okay.

What is knowledge?

Knowledge is when you **understand** something.

It is when you learn a **new skill**, such as playing a sport.

You know someone when you are **familiar** with them.

You learn new things **every day**.

School is important because it **teaches** you to understand.

You can get more knowledge by **reading books**, learning from others or by experiencing new situations.

What is time?

Time is how LONG it takes for something to happen, such as how long you have slept, or how old you are or how many minutes it takes to clean your teeth.

We MEASURE time in different ways. The universe has existed for billions of years. A mayfly lives only for one day.

We tell time using **clocks**.

We use **calendars** to measure days, weeks and months.

It can be different times of the **day and night** in different countries.

Time describes when things happened long ago, or might happen in the **future**.

Time can seem to speed up or slow down. Playtime can be very short. A spelling test can feel as if it will last **forever**.

What are ideas?

Ideas are lots of things.
They can be an OPINION or a thought.
An idea can be what is known about something.
Or it could be the reason to do things.

Ideas can be simple. Let's have fish for dinner.

Ideas can be complicated. Let's work out how to feed all the hungry people in the world.

You can have an idea about what you want to do on holiday...

...but it might be **different** to your best friend's.

The reason for a funny play is to entertain the audience and make them **laugh**.

The reason for this book is to teach young people about **philosophy**.

There are many ideas in the world – the trick is to work out which are the GOOD ones!

What is beauty?

There are many different ideas about beauty.

Some people think that beauty makes you feel EMOTION. You can look at a picture or hear a piece of music which makes you feel happy or sad.

Another way to look at beauty is how SIMILAR an image of an item is to the thing in real life. How close is the apple in the picture to the way a real apple appears?

People **don't always agree** on what is beautiful. That's okay.

Beauty isn't just about what we can **see** or **hear**. Things can also be beautiful if they **taste** delicious, **smell** nice or **feel** good.

Or if something has been **made well**. A handmade jumper can be beautifully knitted.

It's important to remember that beauty is MORE than skin deep. People can be beautiful inside and out.

What should I say?

Words are **powerful**. They let people know what you are thinking.

Saying something can affect people more than you realise. Make sure you choose the right words to say.

It is better to speak the **truth**, but it is also important to work out if it's the right time to do so.

What should I do?

What you DO can show more about how you feel than what you say. So think about how you act, and work out what that shows about your feelings towards your friends and family.

Sharing your toys or your snacks with your friends shows them that you care.

Arguing with your friends tells them that you **don't listen** to their opinions.

Working hard at school shows your teachers that you **want** to do well.

Talking through class tells **your teacher** you don't want to learn.

Helping your parents **tidy up** your bedroom shows them that you respect your home.

Drawing on your bedroom wall shows your parents the **opposite**.

Think how you would FEEL if someone treated you the way you want to treat them, and you'll know what you should do.

So... do we know what philosophy is?

Philosophy asks questions.
We know some of the answers.

We know we should be KIND and think of others.
We know we should always look for the TRUTH.
We know we should APPRECIATE the world around us.
We know what it is to be HUMAN.
We know about TIME and BEAUTY.
We know that we should always keep LEARNING.
We know what we should SAY and what we should DO.

We should never stop asking questions.

If we want to be philosophical
fi-luh-SO-fi-KL
we need to think about the questions
we don't have the answers to.

Why don't you think about some of
the questions you would like answering?

Glossary

Agree	to give your approval, to be alike, to get along well	**Entertain**	providing pleasure for an audience
Appreciate	to see the value of, to be grateful for, to admire, to be fully aware of	**Exercise**	physcical activity that keeps your body fit and healthy
Argue	to discuss different views, to give reasons for or against	**Experience**	living through an event, the skill learned by doing something
Audience	a group of people who watch or listen to something	**Fact**	a piece of information
		Familiar	to know someone well, to have knowledge of something
Believe	to accept something as true, to have as an opinion, to have faith	**Future**	a time that is to come, what is going to happen
Billion	a very large number, worth 1,000 million	**Grateful**	to be thankful, to say thank you for something
Calendar	a chart showing days, weeks and months in a year	**Handmade**	made by hand, or with hand tools
Care	to feel interest or concern for people	**Holiday**	a day with no school or work, a trip spent away from home
Complicated	difficult to understand or explain	**Knitted**	fabric made from wool or cotton using knitting needles
Confident	to feel assured and certain	**Mayfly**	adult insects with fragile wings that only live for a day
Emotion	a strong feeling		

Measure	to record the size or quantity of something	**Similar**	having things in common
Opinion	what you think about someone or something	**Simple**	easy to understand or perform
Opposite	on the other side, end or corner of something, to be as different as possible	**Situation**	events at a particular place and moment
Philosophical	based on philosophy	**Skill**	an ability that comes from training or practice
Planet	a heavenly body that orbits the sun	**Stand up for**	to speak for or act on behalf of someone or something
Play	a story performed on stage	**Support**	to help other people with their goals
Powerful	having power or influence	**Trust**	to believe in someone, to rely or depend on someone or something
React	to act or behave in response to something		
Reason	a statement given to explain something, a good basis	**Unique**	to be the only one of its kind, to be individual
Respect	appreciation for someone or something	**Universe**	everything that is observed or assumed to exist
Share	to use, experience or enjoy with others, to divide equally into portions	**Unselfish**	to be generous with time, money or possessions

www.ingramcontent.com/pod-product-compliance
Lightning Source LLC
Chambersburg PA
CBHW061152070526
44584CB00034B/4494